S.J. GOES HOME

Written by J. C. CARR

Illustrated by KERRI CARABETTA

Author photo: Paul Ostrowski

ISBN: 1478312750
ISBN 13: 9781478312758

Library of Congress Control Number:
2012913616
CreateSpace, North Charleston, SC

DEDICATION

This book is dedicated to the memory of my parents, Nicholas and Alda Carabetta, who, in 1959, gave a home to a lost collie, and, together with me and my three older brothers—Frank, Nicholas and Louis—named him Scotty.

For my Grandmother, Giovanna, who instilled in me love, compassion, and respect for all animals as she taught me to care for Scotty.

For Paul, who happily consented to share his life with me and our dogs, P.J., A.J., and S.J.

For S.J., the greatest dog God ever created and the inspiration for this story.

Hi kids! My name is S.J.

I am a “rough” collie.

Oh! No! They don’t call me rough because I’m rough and tough!

And no! They don’t call me rough because my life as a puppy was rough!

They call me rough because I have long, soft, and very thick, white fur around my neck and on my chest. This extra, thick fur is called my rough.

I am a very handsome boy! Oh! I mean *dog*!

What do you think?

I am also a very happy boy!

Oh! I mean *dog*, again!

I am so happy because I am the luckiest dog on planet Earth!

It is all because of my new mom and dad.

I'll tell you about them later.

PUPPY

Sadly, I was not always so happy and lucky.

I was not always so handsome.

I was not always given the best care.

I did not always live with my new mom and dad.

My name was not always S.J.

In fact, for a long time, I had no name at all.

Would you like to know why?

Yes?

Then let me tell you my story.

A long time ago, I lived with my dog family of collie parents, grandparents, nine brothers and sisters, and many aunts, uncles, and cousins in a place called a puppy mill.

PUPPY MILL
DO NOT ENTER

A puppy mill is a place where too many puppies are born.

Then **more** puppies are born …

and **more and more** puppies are born …

and **still more** puppies are born!

Why are so many puppies born in puppy mills?

I will tell you.

We are born for one reason: *money*.

We are not loved.

We are not cared for.

We are not given to loving families.

We are wanted for one reason: *money*.

MILL

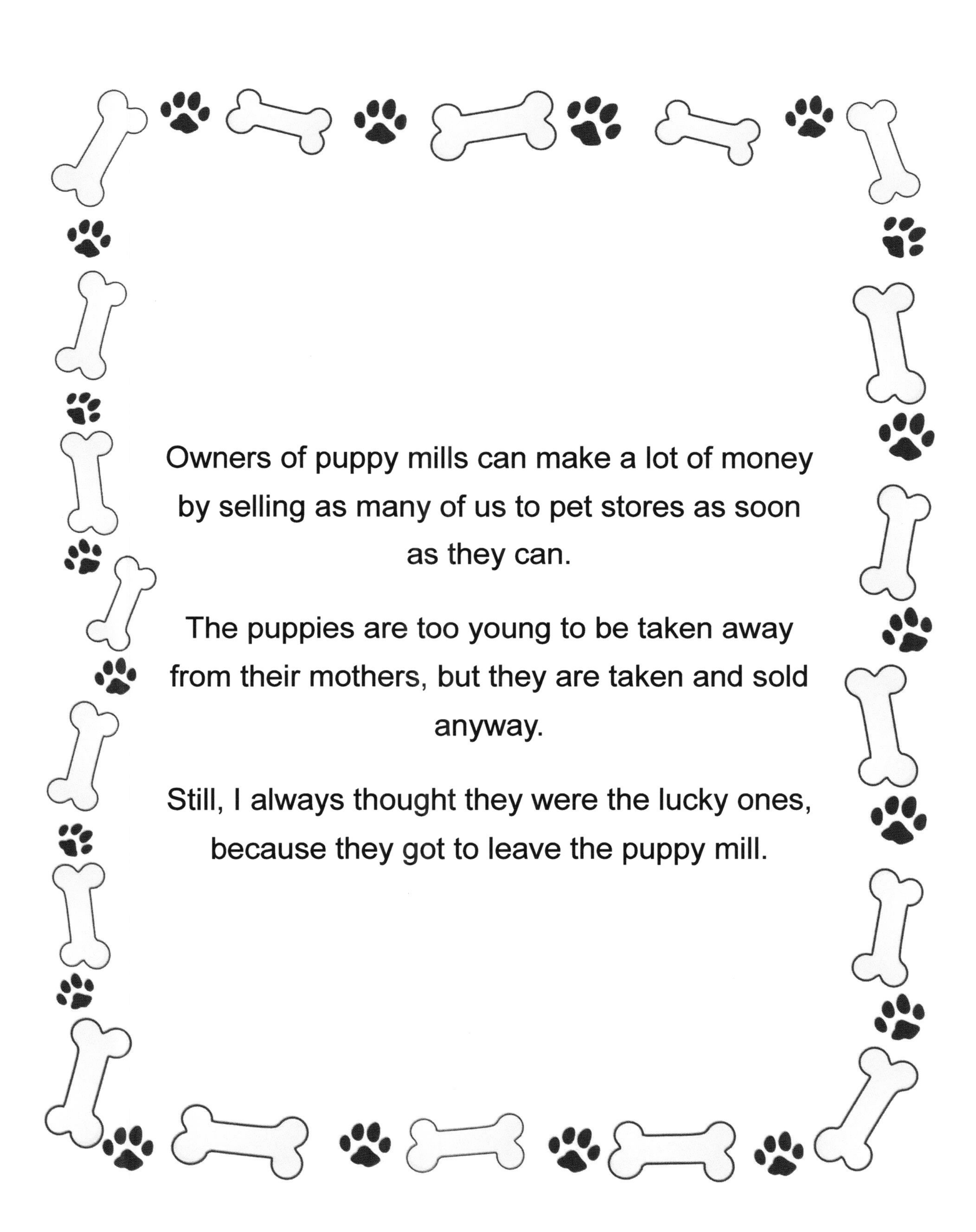

Owners of puppy mills can make a lot of money by selling as many of us to pet stores as soon as they can.

The puppies are too young to be taken away from their mothers, but they are taken and sold anyway.

Still, I always thought they were the lucky ones, because they got to leave the puppy mill.

PUPPY

A puppy mill is a very bad place.

There is no happiness there.

There are no toys to play with.

There are no bones to chew on.

There are no walks to go on.

There are no yards to run in.

In winter, there are no warm beds to curl up in;

In summer, no bowls of cool water to drink from.

There are no families to care for us.

There are no children to love us.

There are only cages …

and **more** cages …

filled with puppies like me.

How do you think we felt?

I will tell you.

We were crammed into filthy cages, and we could hardly move.

We were hot in summer and cold during snowstorms.

We were crying, barking, and howling.

We were hungry and thirsty.

We were scared.

We were sad.

We were tired.

We were miserable.

We wanted to be free.

We wanted a home.

We wanted a family to love us.

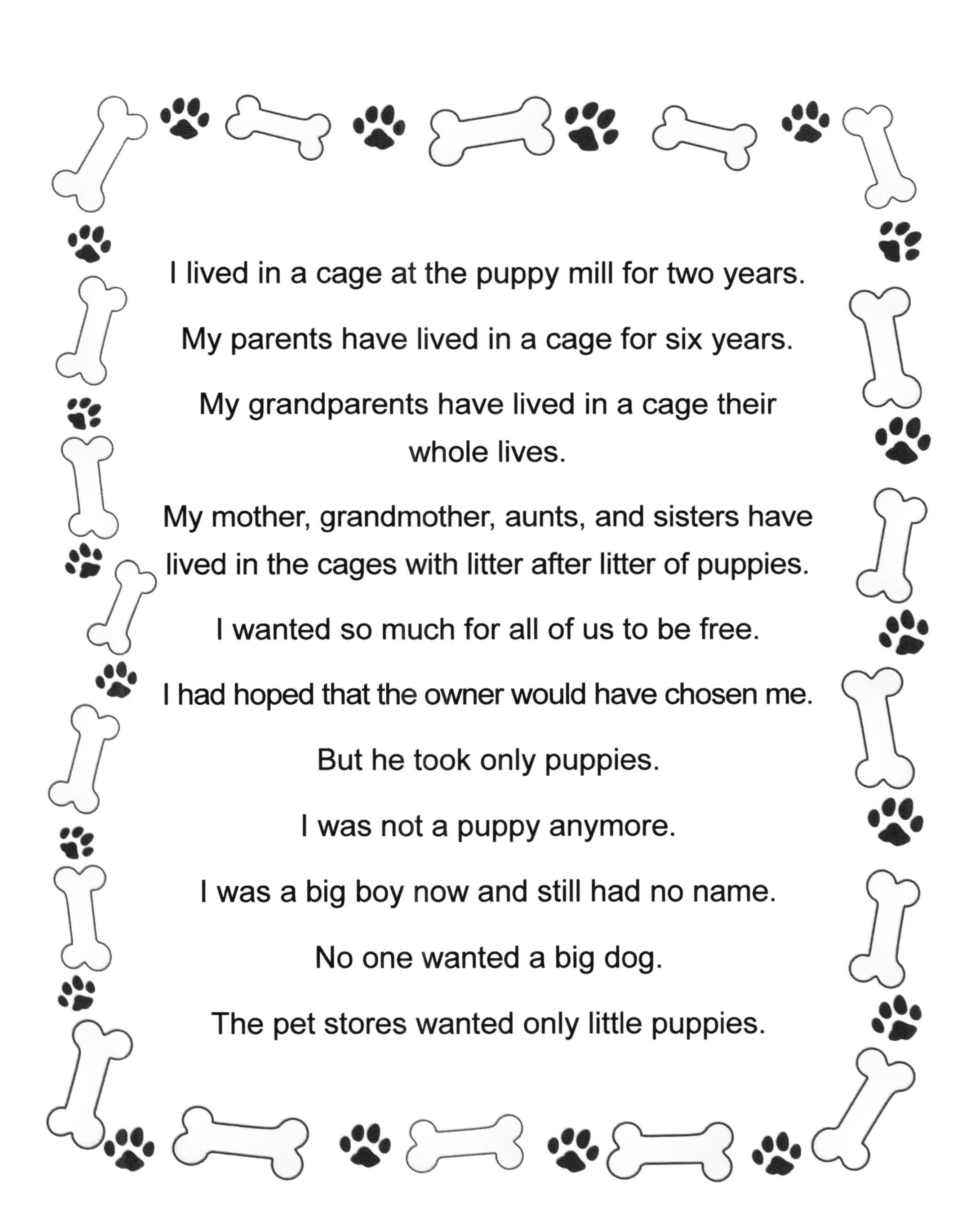

I lived in a cage at the puppy mill for two years.

My parents have lived in a cage for six years.

My grandparents have lived in a cage their whole lives.

My mother, grandmother, aunts, and sisters have lived in the cages with litter after litter of puppies.

I wanted so much for all of us to be free.

I had hoped that the owner would have chosen me.

But he took only puppies.

I was not a puppy anymore.

I was a big boy now and still had no name.

No one wanted a big dog.

The pet stores wanted only little puppies.

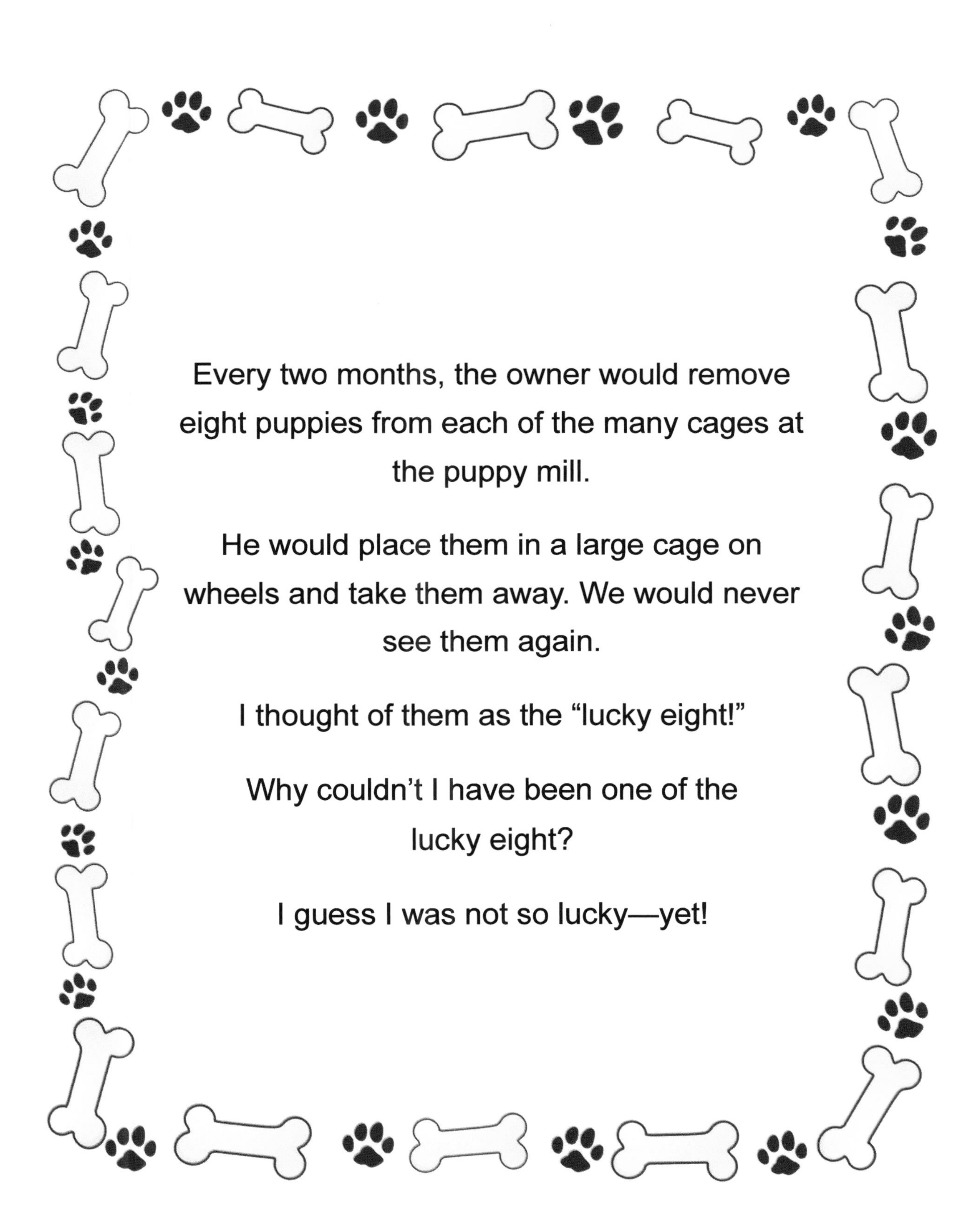

Every two months, the owner would remove eight puppies from each of the many cages at the puppy mill.

He would place them in a large cage on wheels and take them away. We would never see them again.

I thought of them as the “lucky eight!”

Why couldn’t I have been one of the lucky eight?

I guess I was not so lucky—yet!

PUPPY
Animal Helpers

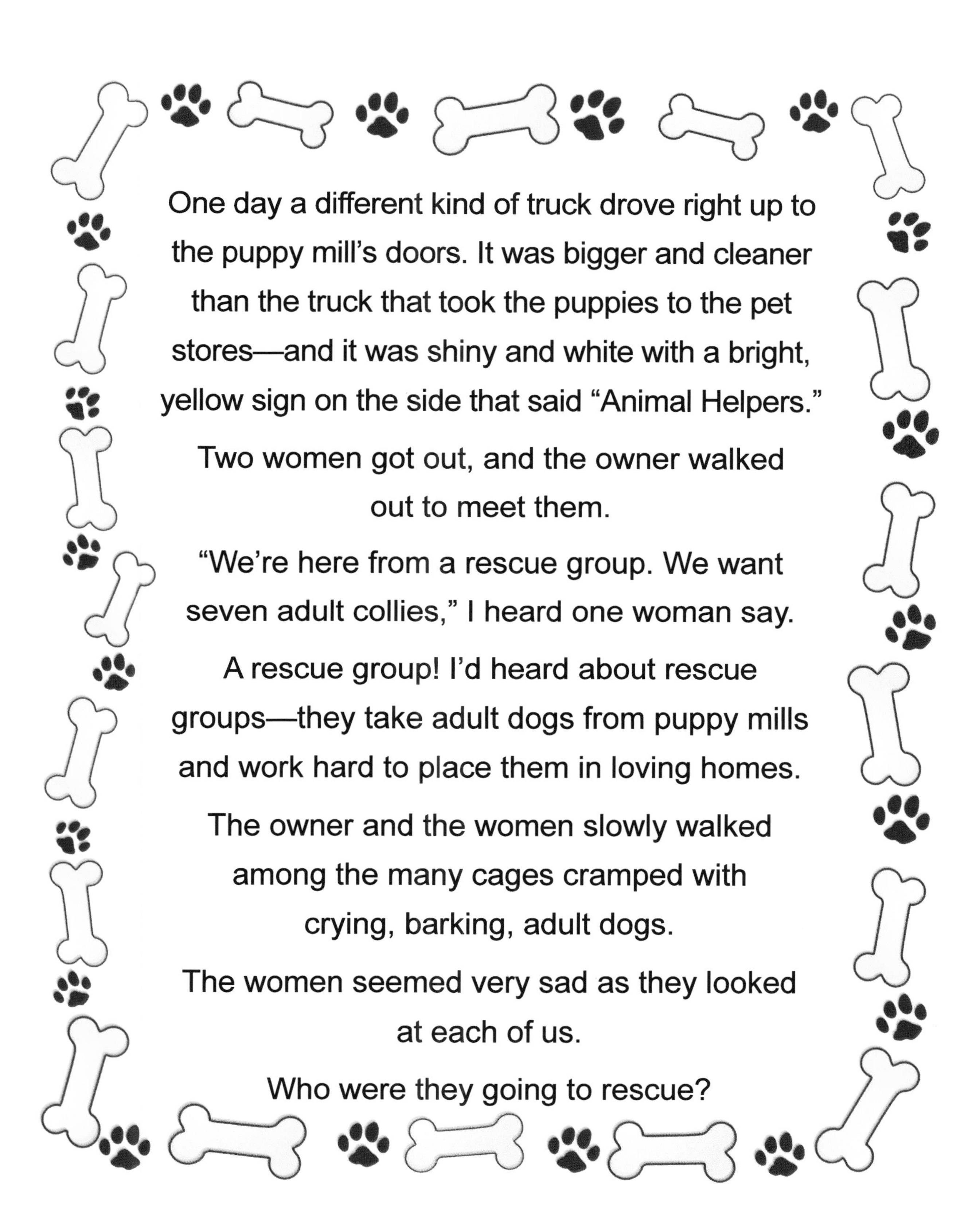

One day a different kind of truck drove right up to the puppy mill's doors. It was bigger and cleaner than the truck that took the puppies to the pet stores—and it was shiny and white with a bright, yellow sign on the side that said "Animal Helpers."

Two women got out, and the owner walked out to meet them.

"We're here from a rescue group. We want seven adult collies," I heard one woman say.

A rescue group! I'd heard about rescue groups—they take adult dogs from puppy mills and work hard to place them in loving homes.

The owner and the women slowly walked among the many cages cramped with crying, barking, adult dogs.

The women seemed very sad as they looked at each of us.

Who were they going to rescue?

HELP

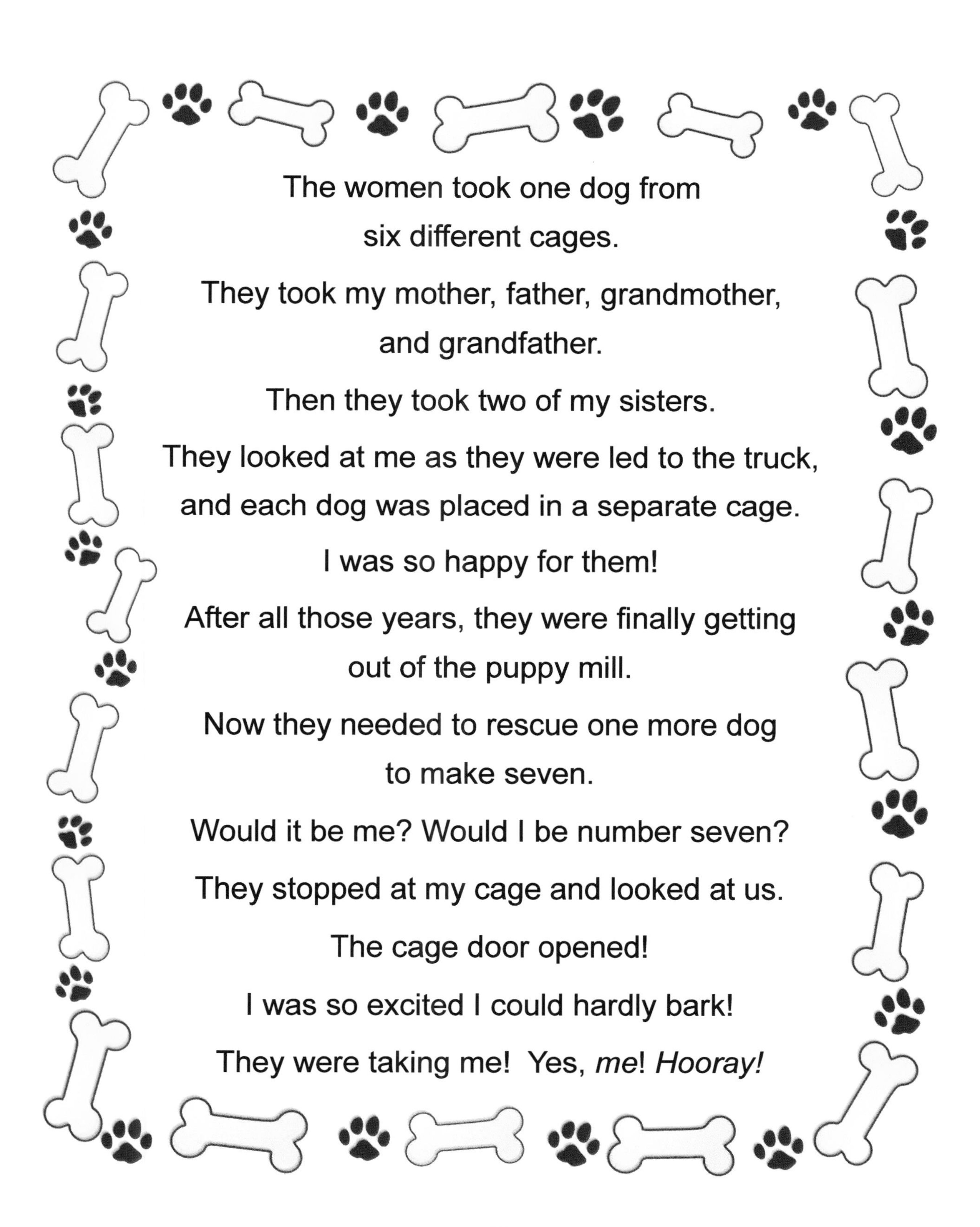

The women took one dog from
six different cages.

They took my mother, father, grandmother,
and grandfather.

Then they took two of my sisters.

They looked at me as they were led to the truck,
and each dog was placed in a separate cage.

I was so happy for them!

After all those years, they were finally getting
out of the puppy mill.

Now they needed to rescue one more dog
to make seven.

Would it be me? Would I be number seven?

They stopped at my cage and looked at us.

The cage door opened!

I was so excited I could hardly bark!

They were taking me! Yes, *me*! *Hooray!*

HELP

Oh!

They did not take me—they took my brother!

I watched as the women rescued my family.

I knew this could be my last chance.

I had to do something!

As the woman closed the cage door,
I placed my paw on her hand.

I looked at her, with my head held high,
loudly barking: “LOOK AT ME!
PLEASE, TAKE ME TOO!”

The woman stopped closing the cage door
and looked into my eyes.

She seemed to understand me.

She yelled out, “Eight! We will take
eight collies today. This one will make eight.”

It was *me*! I was one of the “lucky eight!”

Ready For Adoption Mona Mia
Ready For Adoption Curly
TOWN ANIMAL SHELTER
Ready For Adoption Scotty

After a short ride we were brought to a strange new place called a shelter. A shelter is a place where many kinds of homeless dogs and puppies wait to be adopted by a loving family.

Most of us will wait there for a very long time.

And if more and more puppies are born in puppy mills, there will never be enough homes for all of us!

Sadly, many of us will live our whole lives in a shelter.

A shelter is a better place than a puppy mill; still, only the very lucky will ever find homes.

TOWN
ANIMAL SHELTER
Leash
Adopted
Oreo
Ready For
Adoption
Lucky
Adopted
Jim
Ready For
Adoption
Bo
Adopted
Lucy
Ready For
Adoption
Tye
Adopted
Fifi
Ready For
Rose
Adopted
Lexi
Ready For
Adoption
Rex

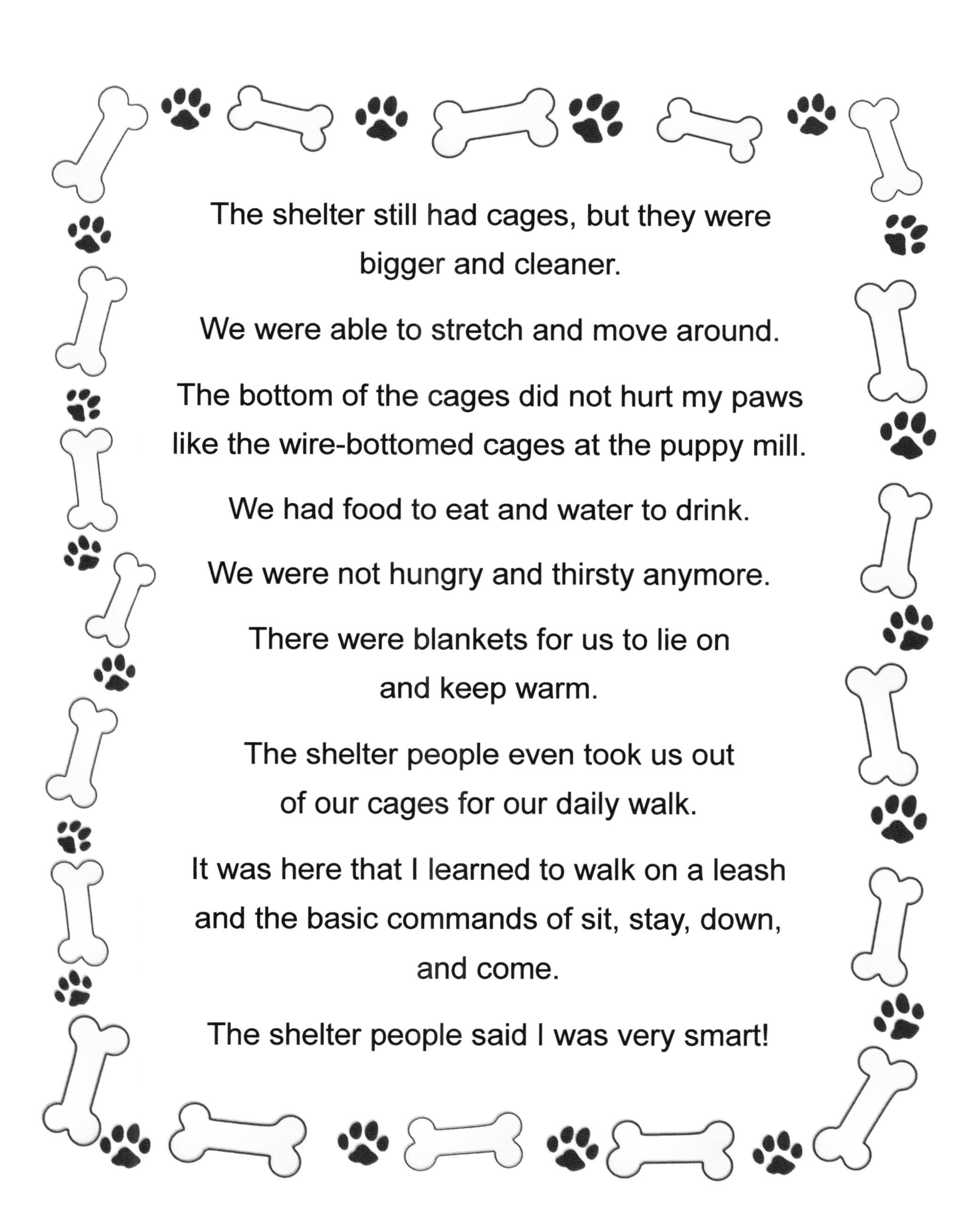

The shelter still had cages, but they were bigger and cleaner.

We were able to stretch and move around.

The bottom of the cages did not hurt my paws like the wire-bottomed cages at the puppy mill.

We had food to eat and water to drink.

We were not hungry and thirsty anymore.

There were blankets for us to lie on and keep warm.

The shelter people even took us out of our cages for our daily walk.

It was here that I learned to walk on a leash and the basic commands of sit, stay, down, and come.

The shelter people said I was very smart!

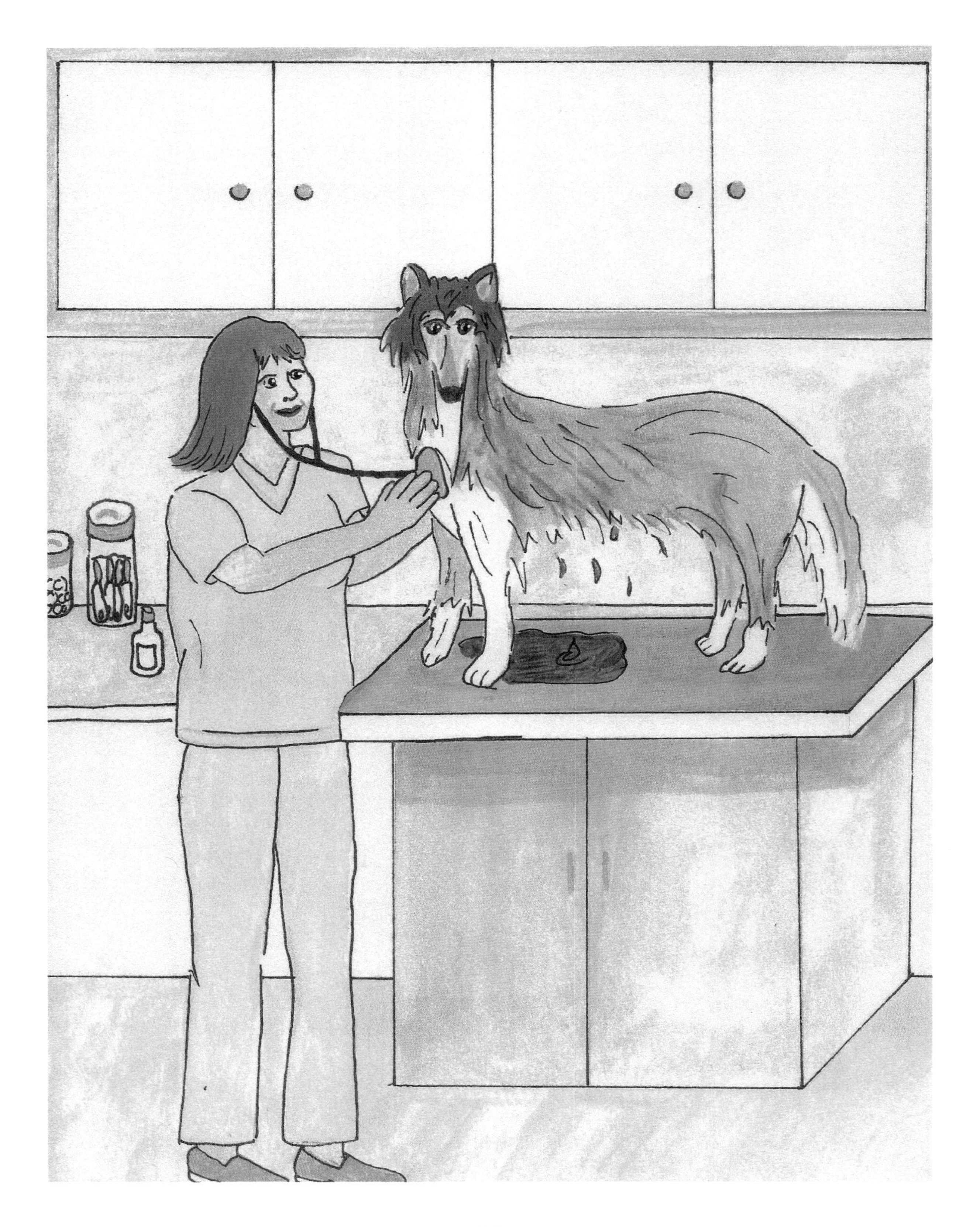

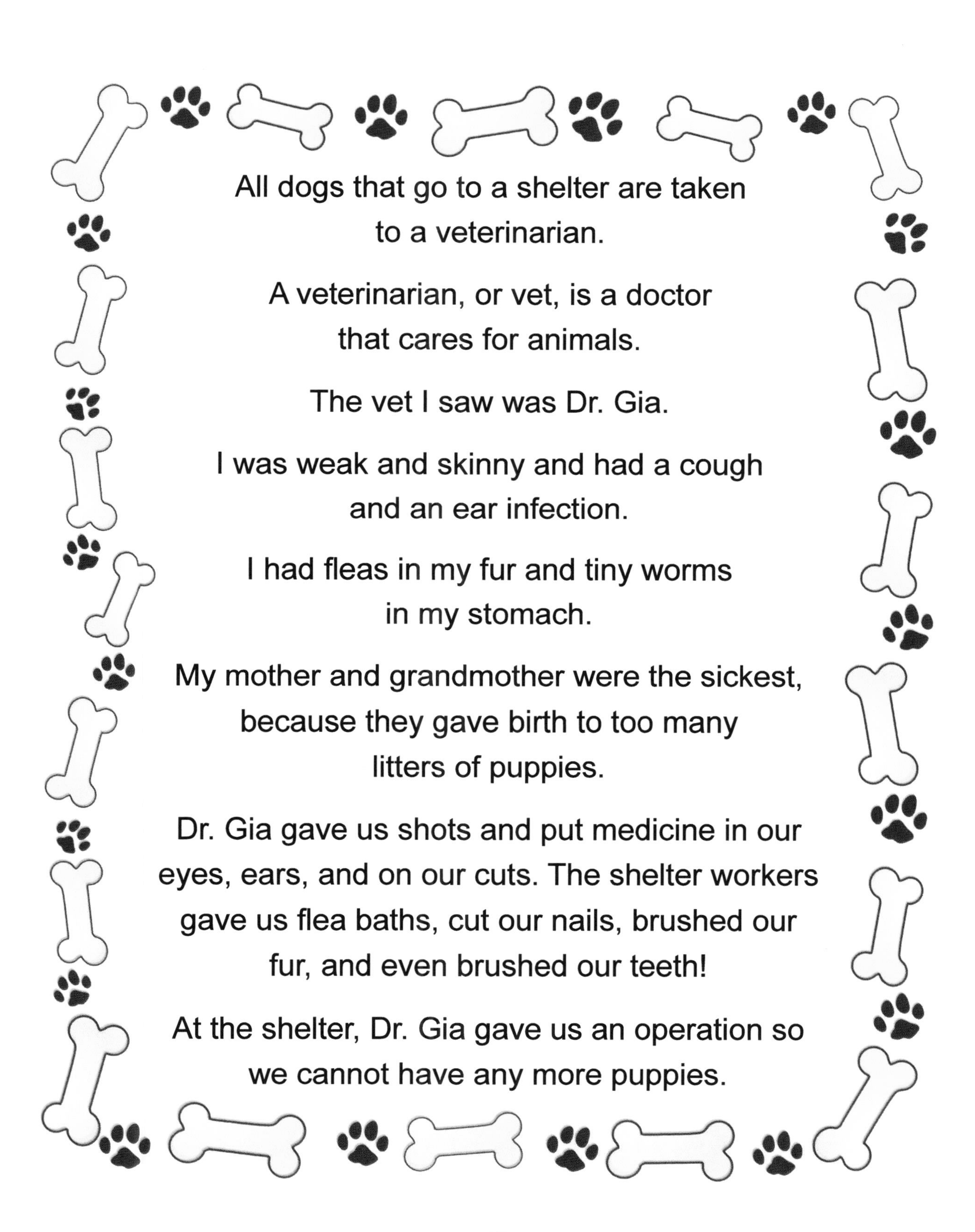

All dogs that go to a shelter are taken
to a veterinarian.

A veterinarian, or vet, is a doctor
that cares for animals.

The vet I saw was Dr. Gia.

I was weak and skinny and had a cough
and an ear infection.

I had fleas in my fur and tiny worms
in my stomach.

My mother and grandmother were the sickest,
because they gave birth to too many
litters of puppies.

Dr. Gia gave us shots and put medicine in our
eyes, ears, and on our cuts. The shelter workers
gave us flea baths, cut our nails, brushed our
fur, and even brushed our teeth!

At the shelter, Dr. Gia gave us an operation so
we cannot have any more puppies.

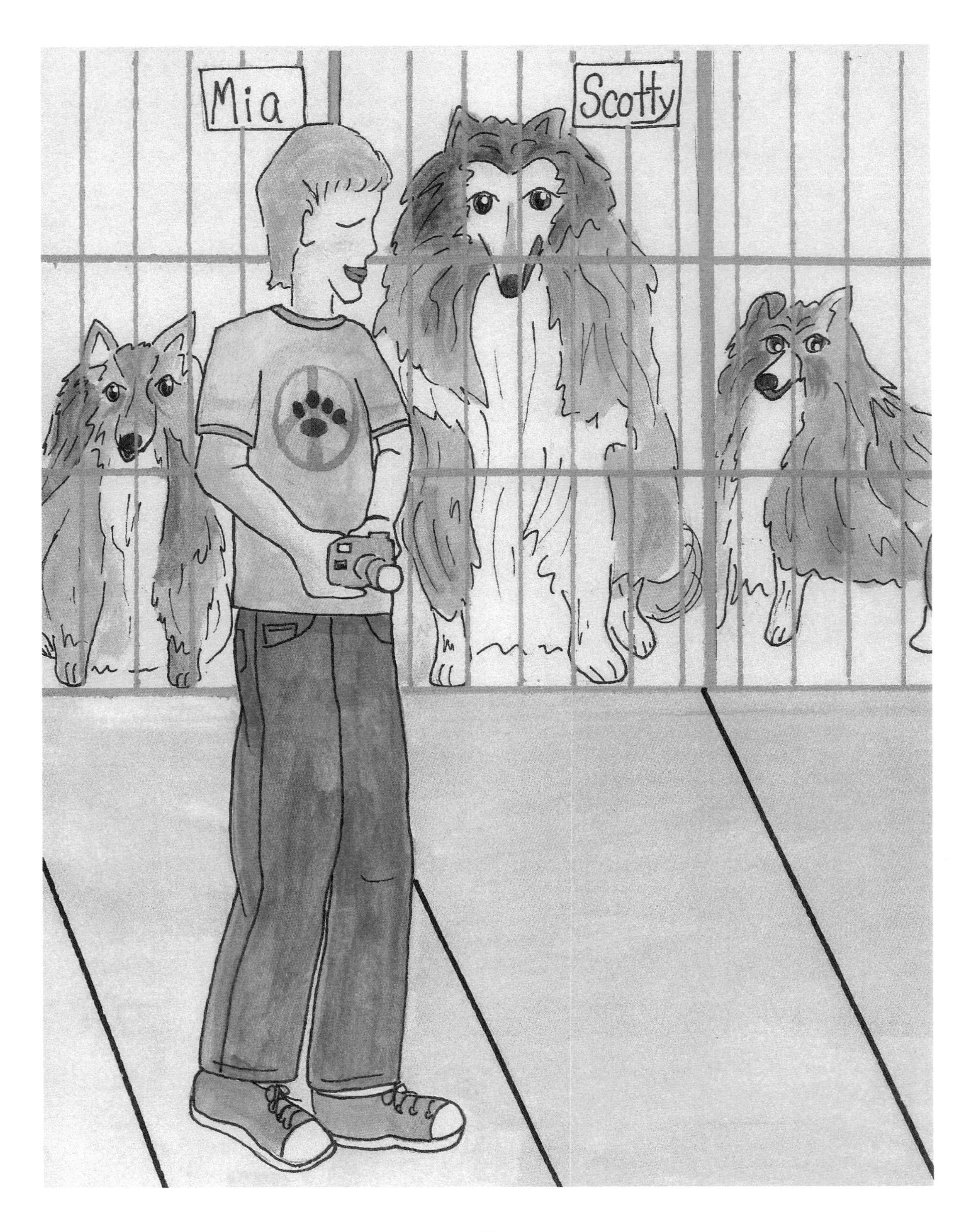
Mia
Scotty

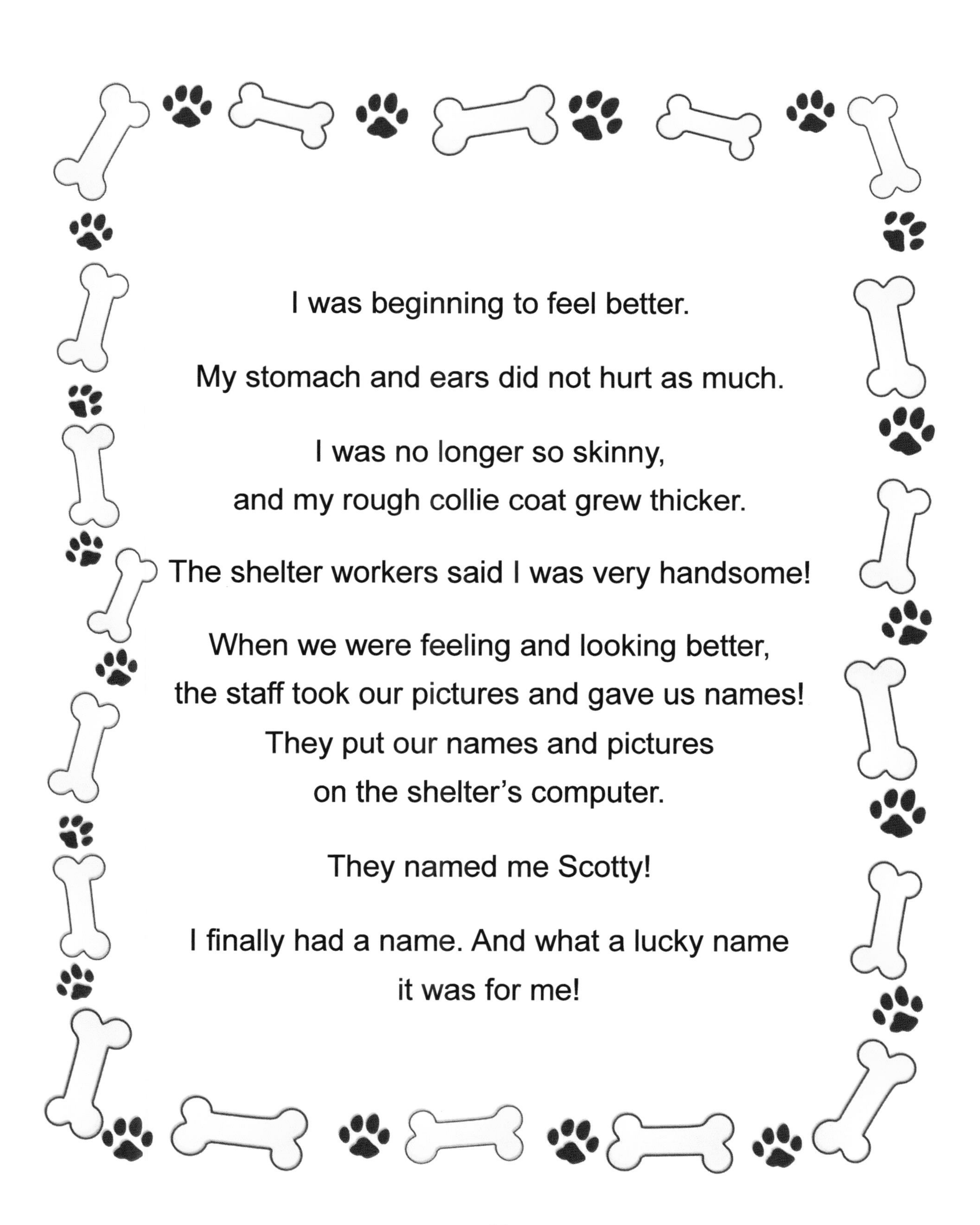

I was beginning to feel better.

My stomach and ears did not hurt as much.

I was no longer so skinny,
and my rough collie coat grew thicker.

The shelter workers said I was very handsome!

When we were feeling and looking better,
the staff took our pictures and gave us names!
They put our names and pictures
on the shelter's computer.

They named me Scotty!

I finally had a name. And what a lucky name
it was for me!

SCOTTY
1959
Wow! look at Scotty! What a beautiful Boy!

Shelters list pictures of all their dogs
on the computer.

People use their computers to see
all the dogs in the shelters.

All you have to do is click on their pictures.

I felt so lucky that people could see
my name and picture!

My mom was looking for a collie to adopt
when she saw *me* on the computer. She knew
immediately I was the one! And it was all
because of my name and picture.

Now, let me tell you about the best part
of my story:

Mom!

As a child, my mom's first pet was also a rough collie. Her parents found him and brought him home.

My mom and her three older brothers named him Scotty!

He was her best friend and constant companion throughout her childhood. It was because of him that my mom developed a lifelong love for collies and a respect for all animals.

Wow! Scotty was my name too!

How lucky could I be?

Animal
Shelter

My mom came to the shelter to meet me.

It was love at first sight.

My mom said, “I want to take him home!”

Then she said to me, “From now on, your name will be S.J.” The *S* is for Scotty and the *J* is for Joni, my mom’s first name. I loved my new name! I felt my mom loved me so much already by giving me a part of her name.

Then mom said, “S.J.! Let’s go home!”

No more puppy mill dog—ever!

No more shelter dog—ever!

I was on my way to a new home and a new life.

And what a life it’s been!

Still, the best is yet to come.

Ready for adoption
Mona
Mia
Ready for adoption Curly
TOWN
ANIMAL SHELT
Adopted
Fred
Ready fur adoption
Patch

How do you think you can help dogs like me?

You can help us by not buying puppies
from a pet store.

You can help us by adopting a dog
from an animal shelter.

You can help us by making sure that your dog
does not give birth to more puppies.

You can help us by telling everyone what
you learned about puppy mills.

You can help us by telling everyone you are
now the proud owner of a rescued, shelter dog!

Just like my mom does!

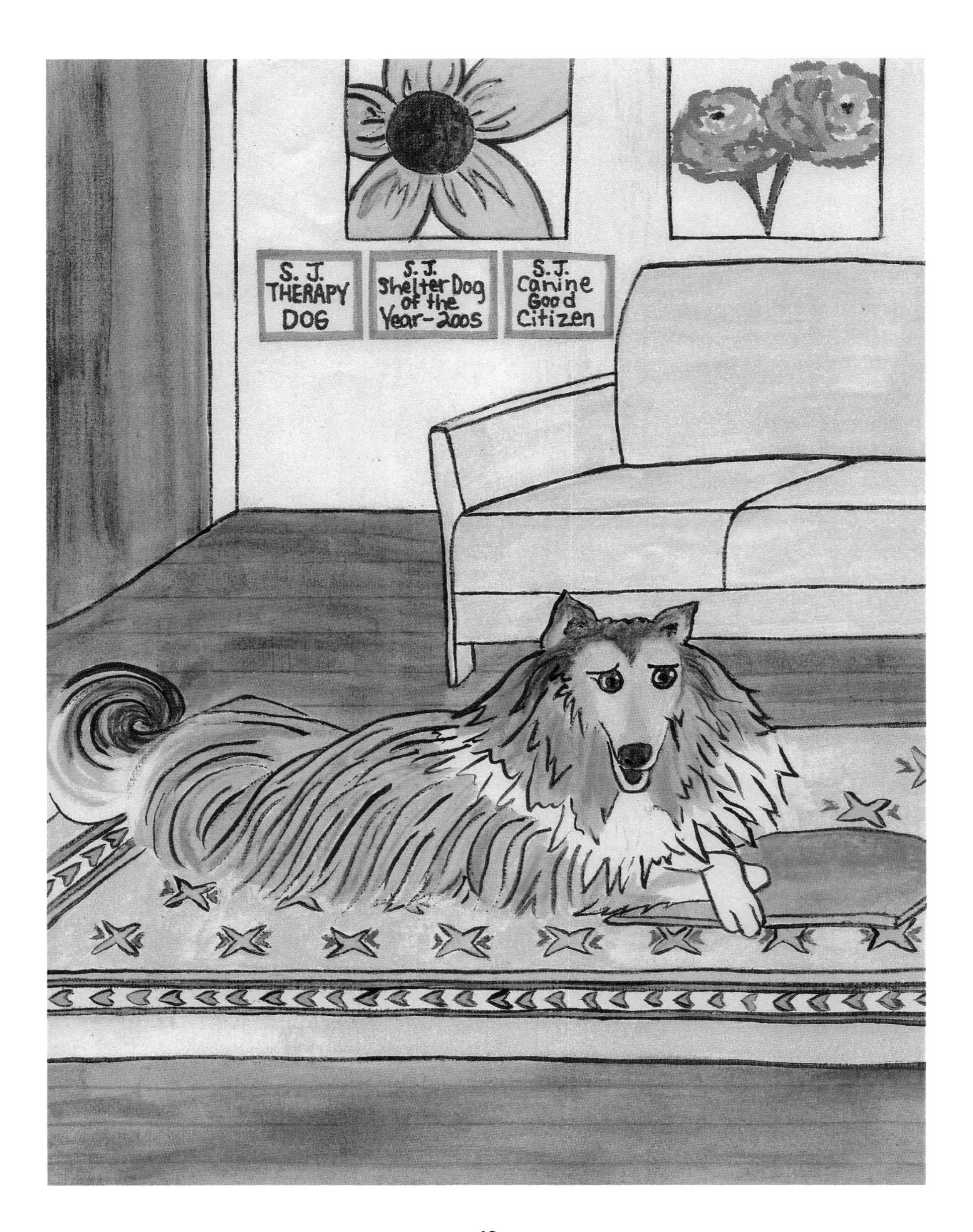
S. J.
THERAPY
DOG
S. J.
Shelter Dog
of the
Year-2005
S. J.
Canine
Good
Citizen

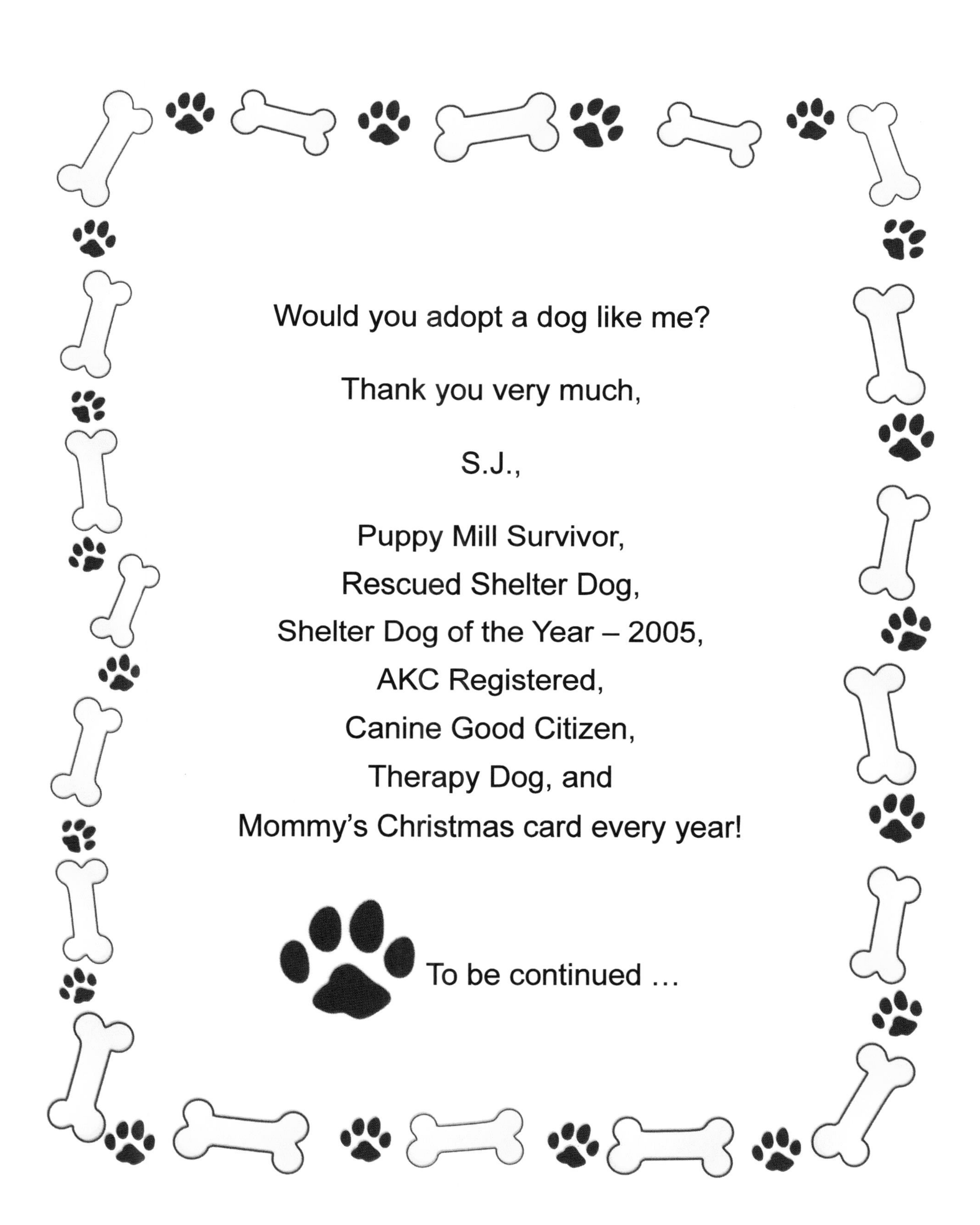

Would you adopt a dog like me?

Thank you very much,

S.J.,

Puppy Mill Survivor,
Rescued Shelter Dog,
Shelter Dog of the Year – 2005,
AKC Registered,
Canine Good Citizen,
Therapy Dog, and
Mommy's Christmas card every year!

To be continued …

ABOUT THE AUTHOR

J.C. Carr is a retired special education teacher who taught in several New York City public and private schools. She holds a Bachelor of Arts degree in English, a Master of Science degree in Secondary Education and New York State certification in Special Education. *S.J. Goes Home*, is based on the true story of her magnificent collie, S.J., formerly Scotty, whom she rescued from an animal shelter in 2002. The book is a realization of a lifelong desire to educate children to the plight of puppy mill dogs, encourage shelter dog adoptions and instill compassion and respect for all animals through humane education.

S.J. was enrolled--- and excelled, in beginner, intermediate, and advanced training courses in obedience school, and achieved certificates and titles to become a certified therapy dog in 2004. He regularly visited a nursing care facility and quickly became a favorite visitor, bringing much joy to the elderly residents, their families and the staff.

J.C. Carr lives in Staten Island, New York, with her husband, Paul, and S.J., where they also raised their first collie, A.J., and their West Highland white terrier, P.J.

ABOUT THE ILLUSTRATOR

Kerrianne Carabetta is a graduate of the Fashion Institute of Technology, where she earned Associate degrees in Fashion Design and Fashion Accessory.

She is a self-employed artist who has been painting murals professionally for businesses and private homes for over a decade. She also teaches painting and creative art projects to children in summer art programs.

The characters in *S.J. Goes Home* are beautifully depicted and brought to life by her vivid, moving illustrations that capture the essence of S.J.'s life.

She lives on the Jersey shore with her husband, Nick, their daughter, Ava, twin sons, Nicholas and Joseph, and their dog, Frankie, a wheaten terrier.

20197438R00033

Made in the USA
Lexington, KY
24 January 2013